Tell M
Another Story,
Sing Me A Song

A One Act Play

by Jean Lenox Toddie

A SAMUEL FRENCH ACTING EDITION

SAMUEL FRENCH

FOUNDED 1830

New York Hollywood London Toronto

SAMUELFRENCH.COM

Tell Me Another Story, Sing Me A Song

THE SCENE. *On a bare stage are six brightly-colored wooden cubes, each approximately two-feet square. Three cubes (red, yellow and blue, respectively) are in place left of center; three cubes of similar color are placed right of center.*

STAGE DIRECTIONS. *As the play opens, two women are sitting on the cubes. The woman, stage left, is the* MOTHER. *The woman, stage right, is the* DAUGHTER. *Age is unimportant; each woman aging about 40 years during the duration of the play. It is suggested they wear yellow tabbards of knee length over blue leotards. They sit, legs crossed, their knees drawn up under their chins. In the first segment the* DAUGHTER *is about five-years-old. The scene is played with the two women looking straight ahead.*

MOTHER. What's the matter?

DAUGHTER. I hear something. There's something in the corner.

MOTHER. Nonsense. There's nothing in the corner.

DAUGHTER. But, Mama, I hear something!

MOTHER. (*With a sigh.*) Alright, we'll turn on the light and take a look. There, you see, there's nothing in the corner. (*Pause.*) Well, is there?

DAUGHTER. I don't know.

MOTHER. Well, how can you see if you don't open

3

your eyes? Open your eyes and look. Is there anything in the corner?

DAUGHTER. (*Dubiously.*) I guess not.

MOTHER. Of course not. And now it's time to climb into bed and say goodnight, isn't it?

DAUGHTER. I guess so.

MOTHER. Goodnight.

DAUGHTER. Mama?

MOTHER. What?

DAUGHTER. Leave the light on.

MOTHER. You won't go to sleep with this light on. But I'll leave the hall light on for awhile. Alright?

DAUGHTER. Alright.

MOTHER. Goodnight.

DAUGHTER. Nite. (*Both women close their eyes, and their heads sink to their knees. After a few seconds, the* DAUGHTER *looks up.*) Mama?

MOTHER. What?

DAUGHTER. Can I have a drink of water?

MOTHER. You had a drink of water.

DAUGHTER. I'm thirsty.

MOTHER. You're not thirsty. How can you be thirsty? You just had a drink of water.

DAUGHTER. But I'm thirsty.

MOTHER. You'll wet your bed.

DAUGHTER. No, I won't.

MOTHER. That's what you said last night.

DAUGHTER. But I won't.

MOTHER. Promise?

DAUGHTER. Cross my heart and point . . .

MOTHER. (*Sharply.*) Better not. Just—promise.

DAUGHTER. Promise.

MOTHER. (*After a pause.*) Here you are. Now, not another peep out of you, you hear?

DAUGHTER. Uh huh.

MOTHER. Well, what do you say?

DAUGHTER. Thank you.

MOTHER. Who?

DAUGHTER. What?

MOTHER. Thank you, who?

DAUGHTER. Thank you, Mama.

MOTHER. You're welcome. Here, give Mama a kiss. That's a good girl. Goodnight, now.

DAUGHTER. Goodnight.

MOTHER. Wait a minute. Did you say your prayers?

DAUGHTER. Uh huh.

MOTHER. On your knees?

DAUGHTER. Uh huh.

MOTHER. (*Pause.*) Did you say your prayers? (*No answer.*) Did you say your prayers or didn't you? (*No answer.*) Alright, young lady, out of bed.

DAUGHTER. Mama . . .

MOTHER. Out of bed and down on your knees.

DAUGHTER. But it's cold.

MOTHER. It wasn't too cold to come wandering into my room asking for a glass of water.

DAUGHTER. But I needed a drink of water.

MOTHER. And now you need to say your prayers. Out of bed.

DAUGHTER. (*Mumbling.*) "Now I lay me . . . "

MOTHER. I can't hear you. If I can't hear you, how can God hear you?

DAUGHTER. (*Speaking louder and faster.*) "Now I lay me down to sleep, I pray the Lord my soul to keep. If I should die before I wake, I pray the Lord my soul to take."

MOTHER. Well! That was nice! Suppose God takes as little time to answer your prayers as you take to say them!

DAUGHTER. Mama, tuck me in.

MOTHER. I'm tucking you in.

DAUGHTER. My feet are cold.

MOTHER. Alright, I'll rub them a minute. There, how's that? (DAUGHTER *murmurs with contentment.*) Give Mama a kiss. That's a good girl. And now, goodnight. (*Again both lower their heads briefly, then* DAUGHTER *raises her head.*)

DAUGHTER. Mama?

MOTHER. What now?

DAUGHTER. Tell me a story.

MOTHER. Your Daddy told you a story.

DAUGHTER. Tell me another story.

MOTHER. No more stories tonight. (*There is another pause.*)

DAUGHTER. Mama?

MOTHER. (*Exasperated.*) What?

DAUGHTER. (*In a small voice.*) Sing me a song.

MOTHER. You're five years old and you're acting like a baby!

DAUGHTER. Please . . .

MOTHER. Alright. If you're going to act like a baby, I'll sing you a baby song. (*As she begins to sing, she is out of patience, but as she continues, her face softens and she is singing to her baby.*)

"Rock-a-bye baby,
On the tree top,
When the wind blows,
The cradle will rock.
When the wind blows,
The cradle will fall,
Down will come baby,
Cradle and all."

(DAUGHTER's *head has lowered, and she is almost asleep.*) Ah, that's a good girl. Here, let me tuck you in. That's mother's good little girl. (MOTHER *slowly lowers her head, too. Then, after a pause, the*

DAUGHTER *slowly raises hers. Wide-eyed, she begins to scan the corners of the room. She has peered into three corners when she seems to hear something. She stiffens and very slowly moves her eyes until she is staring into the last corner. Suddenly, she cries out . . .)*

DAUGHTER. Mama!

MOTHER. (*Sitting up with a jolt.*) What?

DAUGHTER. There's something in the corner of my room!

MOTHER. (*Absolutely exasperated.*) There is nothing in the corner of your room!

DAUGHTER. Mama, there's something in the corner of my room, and I'm scared.

MOTHER. There's nothing in the corner of your room, do you hear? Absolutely nothing. There's nothing to be frightened of. Now I've had just about enough, young lady, now you go to sleep! (*After the* MOTHER's *last words, both women remain motionless for about five seconds, their faces expressionless. Then music commences—"Rock-A-Bye Baby," played with one finger on the piano, or very simply on the guitar, at a sprightly, walking tempo. In time with the music, the women rise, pick up their blue blocks, walk to center stage and place their blocks side by side. They take no notice of each other, but move in unison. Returning to the playing areas, the* DAUGHTER *seats herself on her yellow block, facing stage right, with her feet not quite touching the floor. She is now eight years old.* MOTHER *faces her* DAUGHTER's *back.*) Big girls don't cry.

DAUGHTER. (*Petulantly.*) I'm not a big girl.

MOTHER. Of course you're a big girl. You're in fourth grade. They don't put little girls in fourth grade.

DAUGHTER. I hate fourth grade.

MOTHER. Nonsense, you love it. Why, just the other day you told me you loved your teacher.

DAUGHTER. I don't. I hate her.

MOTHER. Nonsense. Why would you hate your teacher?

DAUGHTER. Because she's an old meanie.

MOTHER. Why, she seems just as nice as she can be.

DAUGHTER. She's a mean old meanie.

MOTHER. Now that's not nice.

DAUGHTER. Well, she is.

MOTHER. Why would she be an old meanie? Something's happened, hasn't it? (DAUGHTER *is silent.*) Hasn't it? Come on, tell Mama what happened.

DAUGHTER. I told you. Everybody got one but me!

MOTHER. But that's because you need more practice.

DAUGHTER. I don't want the dumb old thing anyway.

MOTHER. Well, of course you do. If everyone else in the class has one, you'll want one, too. It's only natural.

DAUGHTER. No I don't neither.

MOTHER. Either.

DAUGHTER. What?

MOTHER. Either. No you don't, either.

DAUGHTER. I already said I don't.

MOTHER. Why do you suppose you need more practice?

DAUGHTER. I don't know.

MOTHER. Your teacher must have said . . .

DAUGHTER. She said because I was left-handed.

MOTHER. Oh?

DAUGHTER. Why am I left-handed? Nobody else in my class is left-handed.

MOTHER. Because you were born that way.

DAUGHTER. Why was I born that way? Nobody else in my class was born that way.

MOTHER. Of course they were.

DAUGHTER. I'm the only one!

MOTHER. That's very strange. There are usually a lot of left-handed children in a class.

DAUGHTER. Well, I'm the only one. My teacher said I was an (*She struggles for the word*) . . . an exception. What's an exception?

MOTHER. It means you're a little different, that's all.

DAUGHTER. But I don't want to be different.

MOTHER. Some day you'll be glad you're different.

DAUGHTER. I hate being different. Why do I have to be different?

MOTHER. Because you were born left-handed.

DAUGHTER. Why?

MOTHER. Probably because I'm left-handed.

DAUGHTER. You're left-handed! (*This is betrayal.*)

MOTHER. You see, you never even noticed. After awhile it won't make any difference. I can do anything anyone else can do.

DAUGHTER. Then why do I need more practice?

MOTHER. Because it's a right-handed world. Left-handed people have to practice to fit into a right-handed world.

DAUGHTER. I wish I was in a left-handed world. I wish I was just like all the other kids in my class.

MOTHER. There is no left-handed world.

DAUGHTER. Why?

MOTHER. There just isn't, that's all, so we have to adjust.

DAUGHTER. I don't want to adjust.

MOTHER. And we have to practice.

DAUGHTER. I don't want to practice.

MOTHER. Well, I'm sorry, but you're going to have to. I had to, and you're going to have to.

DAUGHTER. But I don't want to.

MOTHER. I suggest you stop feeling sorry for yourself, young lady. You have to practice and now is as good a time as any to start. You just sit right down here at the kitchen table and begin. There's a pencil and paper. When I come back I want to see that whole paper filled. (MOTHER *turns to the right, her back to* DAUGHTER, *and stands motionless.* DAUGHTER *swings around to face the audience, and appears to begin to write. As she does, she says softly . . .*)

DAUGHTER. I hate to practice, and I hate my dumb old teacher—and I hate you.

MOTHER. (*Swinging around.*) I heard that! Anymore of that, young lady, and it's off to bed! (*The two women remain motionless for five seconds, then, in time to the music and in unison, they move their yellow blocks stage center and place them on top of the blue blocks. Then they return to their positions—* MOTHER *facing front, with* DAUGHTER *facing her* MOTHER. *In this segment the* DAUGHTER *is 12 years old.*)

DAUGHTER. Can I?

MOTHER. No.

DAUGHTER. Why not?

MOTHER. Because.

DAUGHTER. Because why?

MOTHER. Because you're only 12-years-old, that's why.

DAUGHTER. Everybody else can.

MOTHER. Well, you're not everyone else.

DAUGHTER. Nancy can. Nancy's mother said she could.

MOTHER. Well, I'm not Nancy's mother. If Nancy's mother thinks Nancy's old enough, that's her business. But I'm your mother, and I say "no."

DAUGHTER. (*Wheedling.*) Mom?

MOTHER. No.

DAUGHTER. Ah, Mom . . .

MOTHER. I don't want to hear another word. I've heard all I want to hear.

DAUGHTER. Gee whiz!

MOTHER. All I want to hear.

DAUGHTER. But Mom . . .

MOTHER. One more word and up to your room.

DAUGHTER. But . . .

MOTHER. Another word, and up you go.

DAUGHTER. But Mom . . .

MOTHER. Alright, that's it. *That* is it. I've heard enough. It might be a good idea, young lady, if you went up to your room.

DAUGHTER. That's not fair.

MOTHER. Right this minute.

DAUGHTER. Why can't I? Just tell me why?

MOTHER. Because I said so.

DAUGHTER. But all the other kids can, why can't I?

MOTHER. Up to your room, and stay there until you've learned not to argue with your mother.

DAUGHTER. Everybody but me! What am I supposed to do? And next time they won't even ask me because they'll think I can't go. Because I can never go anywhere.

MOTHER. Up to you room.

DAUGHTER. But . . .

MOTHER. Up to bed, young lady.

DAUGHTER. But I . . .

MOTHER. Not another word. March. (*After five seconds, the music starts and both women pick up*

*their remaining block, carry it center stage and place
it on top of the other two. Now the fence is complete.
Neither woman can see the other. The next segment is
played with both women facing the wall. The DAUGH-
TER is now sixteen.)* So where have you been?

DAUGHTER. What do you mean, where have I been?

MOTHER. Just what I said. Where in the world have
you been?

DAUGHTER. You know where I've been.

MOTHER. Until this hour?

DAUGHTER. What time is it?

MOTHER. What time is it! What time is it! Where's
your watch?

DAUGHTER. I'm not wearing one.

MOTHER. How convenient.

DAUGHTER. Well, what time is it?

MOTHER. Late, that's what time it is. Too late for
a good girl to be out. A good girl would be in bed by
this time. A good girl doesn't keep her mother up
worrying half the night.

DAUGHTER. But you knew I was going to be late.

MOTHER. Not this late! By late I thought you meant
midnight, at most. That's late enough for a sixteen-
year-old girl to be out on the streets.

DAUGHTER. Mom, you might think I was Cinderella.

MOTHER. I wish you were. I wish that at 12 o'clock
you turned back into a daughter who left the shenanigans and came home where she belonged.

DAUGHTER. I'm sorry you were worried.

MOTHER. So where have you been?

DAUGHTER. We got something to eat and then we sat
and talked, that's all.

MOTHER. Where did you sit and talk?

DAUGHTER. If you must know, we were parked right
out there in the driveway.

MOTHER. I knew it! Oh, my God, shenanigans in our driveway! What will the neighbors think?

DAUGHTER. Why should the neighbors know?

MOTHER. I knew, didn't I?

DAUGHTER. How did you know?

MOTHER. She asks me how did I know? At one o'clock in the morning a car pulls into our driveway. Don't you suppose I got up and looked out the window? Don't you suppose the neighbors got up and looked!

DAUGHTER. Why did you ask where I was if you already knew?

MOTHER. I wasn't sure it was you.

DAUGHTER. Who did you think was sitting in the driveway at one o'clock in the morning?

MOTHER. I thought it was you, but I wasn't sure.

DAUGHTER. If you knew I was home, why were you worried?

MOTHER. You weren't home. You aren't home until you're in this house. It was dark out there.

DAUGHTER. It's night. It happens to be dark at night.

MOTHER. Don't be fresh.

DAUGHTER. Oh, Mom . . .

MOTHER. A nice girl doesn't sit in the driveway in the dark.

DAUGHTER. We thought you were asleep. We didn't want to wake you.

MOTHER. What kind of mother can sleep when her sixteen-year-old daughter is out, God knows where, doing God knows what, with God knows who?

DAUGHTER. But you knew I was sitting out in the driveway with the boy I've been going with for two years.

MOTHER. I think you and I better have a talk.

DAUGHTER. Oh, Mom . . .

MOTHER. A talk.

DAUGHTER. Now?

MOTHER. Now.

DAUGHTER. Ah, Mom . . .

MOTHER. You may think you know all there is to know, Miss Smartie, but there are some things you don't know.

DAUGHTER. Alright . . . what?

MOTHER. What do you mean, what?

DAUGHTER. What don't I know?

MOTHER. How should I know what you don't know? Ask me a question and then I'll know.

DAUGHTER. Like what?

MOTHER. Like what you're wondering about.

DAUGHTER. I'm not wondering about anything.

MOTHER. You mean you're only sixteen-years-old, and there's nothing you don't know?

DAUGHTER. I don't know.

MOTHER. (*A pause, then she throws up her hands.*) Alright, alright. Go to bed! (*After five seconds the music begins and the two women walk away from the wall,* DAUGHTER *stage right,* MOTHER *stage left. They turn and face front.*) Oh, my God.

DAUGHTER. I'm sorry I told you.

MOTHER. Oh, my God.

DAUGHTER. Mom, it's not that bad.

MOTHER. Not that bad!

DAUGHTER. No, it's not that bad. I'm not the only one. It happens. It happens to lots of girls.

MOTHER. Not to my daughter!

DAUGHTER. Look, I'm no different than anyone else. It could happen to me, and it did. And anyway, it's nothing so terrible. I'm 21 years old.

MOTHER. She says it's nothing so terrible!

DAUGHTER. It's not, Mom, not anymore.

MOTHER. It's a terrible thing. In the eyes of God it's a terrible thing, and what will the neighbors say? Nothing you or any other smart young person says is going to make it alright.

DAUGHTER. How do you know how God looks at things? Maybe God has grown up, too.

MOTHER. What about your father? This is going to kill him.

DAUGHTER. Why does he have to know?

MOTHER. Because he's your father, that's why.

DAUGHTER. But if it hurts him, why tell him?

MOTHER. Why tell me? Don't you think it hurts me? So why tell me? Because I'm your mother, that's why.

DAUGHTER. (*With head lowered, she says softly.*) Mama . . .

MOTHER. What?

DAUGHTER. (*Crying now.*) Mama . . .

MOTHER. (*She does not see her* DAUGHTER, *but senses what is happening.*) What's the matter? Are you crying? (*She walks toward the wall.*)

DAUGHTER. I'm not crying.

MOTHER. We'll just see. (*Removing the top block, she looks over the wall.*) Come here. Come over here. (DAUGHTER, *still looking down, walks slowly to the wall.*) Look at me. (DAUGHTER *raises her eyes. This is the first time in the play that the two women have looked at each other and really seen each other.*) You're crying.

DAUGHTER. Oh, Mama, what am I going to do?

MOTHER. (*She reaches over and, very gently, touches her* DAUGHTER's *hair.*) It's alright, it's alright. It's going to be alright. After all, it's nothing so terrible.

DAUGHTER. It's the worst thing that could have happened. (*She lowers her head.*)

MOTHER. (*She reaches over the wall and raises her* DAUGHTER's *chin.*) Nonsense, it's not the worst thing that could have happened. We're alive, aren't we? We'll work it out.

DAUGHTER. Mama?

MOTHER. Hush now. You go on upstairs. Your bed's made up. You'll stay here tonight.

DAUGHTER. I should go back to the apartment.

MOTHER. Hush now, you'll stay here. Go on up. There's a nightgown in the drawer. I'll be up in a minute, I'm going to make some cocoa.

DAUGHTER. I don't think I want anything, Mom.

MOTHER. We could both use some cocoa. It will help us sleep.

DAUGHTER. Oh, Mom . . .

MOTHER. We'll talk about it tomorrow. We'll talk after a good night's sleep.

DAUGHTER. Oh, Mom, I won't be able to sleep.

MOTHER. A little cocoa, you'll be surprised. Then, in the morning, we'll all sit down and talk.

DAUGHTER. You're going to tell Papa!

MOTHER. Of course we're going to tell him. We're a family, aren't we?

DAUGHTER. You said it would kill him.

MOTHER. Nonsense, it won't kill him. Why should it kill him? He's a grown man, isn't he?

DAUGHTER. I don't want to upset him.

MOTHER. He's your father and he loves you. He has a right to know. Don't worry, we'll work it out. Has there ever been anything we couldn't work out? Go on up, now. I'll make the cocoa. It won't take a minute. When you were a little girl, you always liked your cocoa, remember?

DAUGHTER. Mama? (*She reaches across the wall to her* MOTHER.) Thank you.

MOTHER. (Patting her DAUGHTER's *hand, she says softly.*) Now go to bed. (*Both* MOTHER *and* DAUGHTER *pick up blocks that topped the wall and return with them, in time to the music, to their original positions.* MOTHER *sits on her block.* DAUGHTER, *arms folded, stands looking down at her* MOTHER. *The* DAUGHTER *is now about age thirty.*)

DAUGHTER. You're spoiling him.

MOTHER. Nonsense. He's just a little frightened, that's all. Children are afraid of the dark now and then.

DAUGHTER. He was trying to get your attention and he succeeded. He knows very well there's nothing in the corner. We go through that routine every night. It's his way of getting someone to sit with him.

MOTHER. There's no harm in sitting here for awhile.

DAUGHTER. (*With tenderness.*) Not for you. You're happy as a clam. But what about me? You're going home tomorrow and I have to live with him for the next week. He'll drive me wild—"Can I have a drink of water, tell me another story, sing me a song."

MOTHER. All children like to hear a story before they go to sleep.

DAUGHTER. One story, but not a string of them. One is enough.

MOTHER. Not always.

DAUGHTER. And enough water to do the dead man's float?

MOTHER. What's the matter with a couple of glasses of water?

DAUGHTER. He'll wet his bed.

MOTHER. So wash the sheets.

DAUGHTER. Oh, Mom, you're getting worse all the time. You're an old softie.

MOTHER. So, I'm an old softie.

DAUGHTER. You know what? It's not him, it's you. You encourage him because you like sitting here in the dark.

MOTHER. There are worse places to be than with your grandson.

DAUGHTER. (*Lightly.*) If Papa were here, you wouldn't spend all your time being a professional grandmother.

MOTHER. (*Sighs.*) Well, your father's not here. And anyway, I happen to like the profession.

DAUGHTER. But you're tired, Mom. You've had a long day.

MOTHER. At my age you get a little tired after a day at the zoo.

DAUGHTER. Is he asleep?

MOTHER. (*Looking down and smiling.*) He's asleep. (*She bends over.*) Grandma's little fellow's fast asleep.

DAUGHTER. Alright now. It's time Grandma got some sleep. You've a plane to catch tomorrow. Come on, old softie, go to bed. (*The two women walk to the wall, in time to the music, and remove the second blocks, returning them to their original positions.* MOTHER *sits on her blocks, facing front, feet flat on the floor, head bent, hands folded. She is an old lady.* DAUGHTER *looks at her* MOTHER *with concern. She walks to the wall, picks up the one remaining block, places it next to the old woman and sits down.*) Everything alright, Mom?

MOTHER. (*Without raising her head.*) Everything's fine.

DAUGHTER. Seem a little strange?

MOTHER. I slept in the same bed for 55 years, 40 of them with your father.

DAUGHTER. I know, Mom, but you'll get used to it here. You're going to like it here.

MOTHER. I never wanted to be a burden.

DAUGHTER. What burden?

MOTHER. I wanted to stay in my own house.

DAUGHTER. I know, Mom, and you did, for as long as you could. We were so proud of you, taking care of that big place, shoveling the driveway last winter . . .

MOTHER. I never wanted to be a burden.

DAUGHTER. Mama, you're not a burden.

MOTHER. I'll be a bother, you wait and see.

DAUGHTER. Mama, you won't be a bother.

MOTHER. You'll see. Two women in the same house is a bother. I'll get on your nerves.

DAUGHTER. (*Smiling.*) That's nothing new. We always got on each other's nerves. But Mama, we've always worked things out, haven't we?

MOTHER. You're a good girl.

DAUGHTER. I'm a peach.

MOTHER. No, I mean it, you're a good girl.

DAUGHTER. Mama, we're glad to have you here. This is where you belong. We're a family, remember? (*She pats her* MOTHER's *hand.*) Here, let me tuck you in. (DAUGHTER *picks up her block, carries it to her side of the stage, places it in its original position and sits down. Both women look straight ahead, faces gentled by the years.*) Mom?

MOTHER. Yes?

DAUGHTER. Everything alright?

MOTHER. Everything's alright.

DAUGHTER. Good, so go to sleep. (*As the music plays, very softly, both women draw their knees up under their chins and lower their heads to their original positions. Lights lower.*)

THE END

FLOOR PLAN OF SET:

The stage is bare except for six brightly-colored wooden cubes, each approximately two-feet square. The cubes (red, yellow and blue, respectively) are placed in sets of three, right and left of center stage.

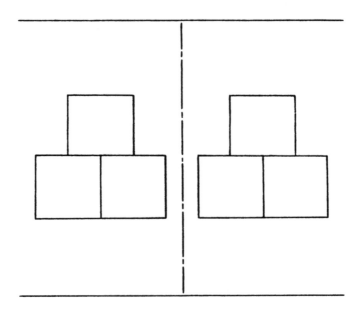

There are no properties used in the play.

Also By
Jean Lenox Toddie

A BAG OF GREEN APPLES

A LITTLE SOMETHING FOR THE DUCKS

AND GO TO INNISFREE

AND SEND FORTH A RAVEN

BY THE NAME OF KENSINGTON

IS THAT THE BUS TO PITTSBURGH?

THE JUICE OF WILD STRAWBERRIES

LATE SUNDAY AFTERNOON, EARLY SUNDAY EVENING

LOOKIN' FOR A BETTER BERRY BUSH

SCENT OF HONEYSUCKLE

THOSE SINGING SUNDAY MORNINGS

WHITE ROOM OF MY REMEMBERING

SAMUELFRENCH.COM

OTHER TITLES AVAILABLE FROM SAMUEL FRENCH

THREE YEARS FROM "THIRTY"
Mike O'Malley

Comic Drama / 4m, 3f / Unit set

This funny, poignant story of a group of 27-year-olds who have known each other since college sold out during its limited run at New York City's Sanford Meisner Theater. Jessica Titus, a frustrated actress living in Boston, has become distraught over local job opportunities and she is feeling trapped in her long standing relationship with her boyfriend Tom. She suddenly decides to pursue her dreams in New York City. Unbeknownst to her, Tom plans to propose on the evening she has chosen to leave him. The ensuing conflict ripples through their lives and the lives of their roommates and friends, leaving all of them to reconsider their careers, the paths of their souls and the questions, demands and definition of commitment.

OTHER TITLES AVAILABLE FROM SAMUEL FRENCH

THE RIVERS AND RAVINES
Heather McDonald

Drama / 9m, 5f / Unit Set
Originally produced to acclaim by Washington D.C.'s famed
Arena Stage. This is an engrossing political drama about the
contemporary farm crisis in America and its effect on rural
communities.

"A haunting and emotionally draining play. A community of
farmers and ranchers in a small Colorado town disintegrates
under the weight of failure and thwarted ambitions. Most of
the farmers, their spouses, children, clergyman, banker and
greasy spoon proprietress survive, but it is survival without
triumph. This is an *Our Town* for the 80's."
– *The Washington Post*

Lightning Source UK Ltd.
Milton Keynes UK
UKHW021431081121
393609UK00013B/210